To the memory of my lovely grandad Percy and my uncle David.

And for my brave, kind, and wonderful dad, who was and will always be my guiding light xx

A Note About This Story

The Beach Village of this tale once stood on the coast of Suffolk in England, where it was home to a thriving fishing
community for more than one hundred years. Every year for the "home fishing" season, which lasted from October to early winter,
hundreds of Scotch fisher-girls and men were welcomed to the village to help pack and pickle the fish.
During the November full moon, everyone worked as hard as they could, as it was believed the full moon would bring
the biggest, best catch—this moon was known as the herring moon.

After major flooding and two world wars, the people of the village saw their way of life change. Many fishermen lost their boats
in the wars, and their houses were damaged. The great floods in 1953 were the final blow for Beach Village.
The few fishing folk left had to leave their homes. It was the end of Beach Village, but its legacy is remembered
by those who grow up fishing and baking and living on the coast of Suffolk—including the creator of this book.

First US edition 2022
First published by Templar Books, an imprint of Bonnier Books UK, 2022

Library of Congress Catalog Card Number 2021953475
ISBN 978-1-5362-2389-7

22 23 24 25 26 27 TLF 10 9 8 7 6 5 4 3 2 1

Printed in Dongguan, Guangdong, China

This book was typeset in Adobe Caslon Pro.
The illustrations were done in pencil and ink.

TEMPLAR BOOKS
an imprint of
Candlewick Press
99 Dover Street
Somerville, Massachusetts 02144

www.candlewick.com

The BAKER by the SEA

PAULA WHITE

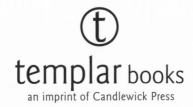

templar books
an imprint of Candlewick Press

If you keep walking over the hills . . .

and across the fields . . .

you will come to the edge, where the land meets the sea.

And on this edge, where the beach begins,
lies a village.

This is my home.

Our home, our Beach Village by the sea.

We have fish merchants,
smokers that smoke the fish,
blacksmiths and basket-makers,
butchers and bakers.
There are cozy cafés and
tiny shops that sell everything
you might need.

Everyone works hard by the sea.
The sailmakers make sails and the boatbuilders build
and mend the boats so that the fishermen can go to sea.
The net-makers make nets and the rope-makers make rope
so that the fishermen can catch the fish.
The coopers make the barrels for pickling,
and the Scotch fisher-girls prepare, pack, and pickle the fish.

The sea is the beating heart of all we do.

As the sun sets slowly behind the cliff, the weary workers make their way home, and the village begins to rest.

And at night, while the fishermen are fishing, the village
lies sleeping, gently soothed by the rhythm of the sea.

In the quiet, I think of the hardworking people
still outside in the cold and rain.

When I am older, I am going to be a fisherman.
I will brave the waves and windy weather
and catch the finest and freshest fish
for the people of the village by the sea.

On the boat we will work together,
handling, hoisting, and heaving the ropes,
ready for our biggest catch.

When the wind begins to whistle, the sky turns inky black,
and waves as tall as houses come crashing down, we will know what to do—
for we bold fishermen can battle any storm.

And when we head for home as the sea starts to calm and
a heavy blanket of fog rolls in, we will search for the bright white light
high on the cliff and listen for the bellow of the foghorn.

We will steer safely home—home to our village,
where the land meets the sea.

My father is not a fisherman.

He is the baker. Every day before the sun rises
and the boats come in, he is safe and warm inside,
busily baking. The comforting aroma of fresh bread
welcomes a new day.

He bakes bread,

buns,

and biscuits.

He bakes baskets of bread for Babs' Corner Café,

where Babs makes the best bacon butties, the boatbuilders' favorite.

He delivers bags of piping hot buns
for the tough Scotch fisher-girls.

And he sells boxes of biscuits

for the brave fishermen to take to sea.

Sometimes I help my father, and as the glow from the oven
keeps us toasty and warm, I think of all the people working outside
in the wet and windy weather.

I wonder, if my father could have made barrels or built boats . . .
why did he choose to be just a baker?

And I ask him,
"Have you ever been to sea?"

"Yes," he replies. "When I was a boy.
I tried it once and even twice and
I knew it wasn't for me."

He pats his apron,
and a floury cloud fills the air.
I see his pride shine through.

"I became a baker, son.
It's what I wanted to do."

"Just imagine if there were no bread, buns, or biscuits.
What would the boatbuilders do if Babs served
breadless bacon butties at the Corner Café?
Or if the Scotch fisher-girls, out in the open in the bitter cold,
didn't get the piping hot buns that warm their nimble fingers?
The fish would pile up, with no room for more."

"And what would happen to the fishermen who fish until dawn,
without their biscuits dipped in hot broth and dunked in their tea?

They would be too cold and hungry to catch the fish
out in the dangerous sea."

But everyone has had their fill today, their bellies warm inside.
And with the boats safely home, the harbor comes to life, busy and bustling
with lifting and lugging, as the fishermen unload the precious catch.

As the morning sun climbs higher in the sky,
a tired fisherman stops by.
He looks to my father and they share weary smiles.

Then, without a word,
he passes my father the finest and fattest fish,
with a thankful glint in his eye.

I look at my father and feel proud.

For without the bread, buns, and biscuits
that he busily bakes before the sun rises,
the people of the village could not
go on as they do.

When I am older, I am going to be a baker
in the village by the sea.

For everyone works hard here.
Everyone, including me.